GEORGE and his
GIANT SHADOW

For Betsey

Library of Congress Cataloging-in-Publication Data
Severn, Jeffrey.
   George and his giant shadow / text and illustrations by Jeffrey
Severn.
      p.   cm.
      Summary: George's giant shadow always gets in the way and
alienates him from his friends until, with the help of his shadow, he
performs an act of bravery that wins his friends back forever.
      ISBN 0-87701-634-8
      [1. Shadows—Fiction.   2. Mice—Fiction.]   I. Title.
   PZ7.S5156Ge   1989   89-932
   [E]—dc19   CIP
                                                                        AC

Many thanks to Diane Goldsmith and all my friends at
Square Moon Productions
for their enthusiasm, support, and helpful advice.

10 9 8 7 6 5 4 3 2 1

Chronicle Books
275 Fifth Street
San Francisco, California 94103

GEORGE and his GIANT SHADOW

WORDS AND PICTURES BY JEFFREY SEVERN

CHRONICLE BOOKS · SAN FRANCISCO

George was different from all the other mice. He had a giant shadow.
No matter where George went, his giant shadow would cause trouble.

When the mice played hide and seek, George was much too easy to find.

When George went with the other mice to the beach, his giant shadow made them shiver.

George tried everything to get rid of it.
He tried hiding in a teacup, but that didn't work.

He tried wearing a disguise, but that didn't work.

He tried losing weight, but that didn't work either.

No matter what George did, his giant shadow just wouldn't go away.

One day, the mice planned an expedition to the pantry.
They mapped out every detail.
They would travel to the kitchen and load up
their knapsacks with their favorite foods:
sunflower seeds, peanuts, oatmeal, and raisins.

All the mice were going—except George.
"Sorry George," the others said. "You can't come.
You and your giant shadow will just be in the way."

George felt very sad. He went to his room to think about his troubles.
He wondered if he and his giant shadow would EVER have any friends.

Slowly the day turned to twilight, and the twilight to night.
It got darker and darker and darker,
until it was so dark that George couldn't even see his giant shadow.

He put on his knapsack and hurried off to tell the others.

Meanwhile, on the other side of the house,
the mice were making their way toward the pantry.
They climbed over the couch.

They chopped their way through a jungle of potted plants.

They tunneled beneath the rug.

Until, at last, they came to the kitchen.

It was there George found his friends.
They were too busy to notice George,
and they were too busy to notice the danger lurking in the dark.
George realized that something terrible was about to happen!
He quivered with fear, but George knew he had to save the other mice.

The danger crept closer. And closer. And closer.

Suddenly, George remembered what he had come
to tell the other mice, and that gave him an idea.
Quickly, he swung into action.
He climbed up the chair, grabbed the light chain,
and pulled with all his strength.

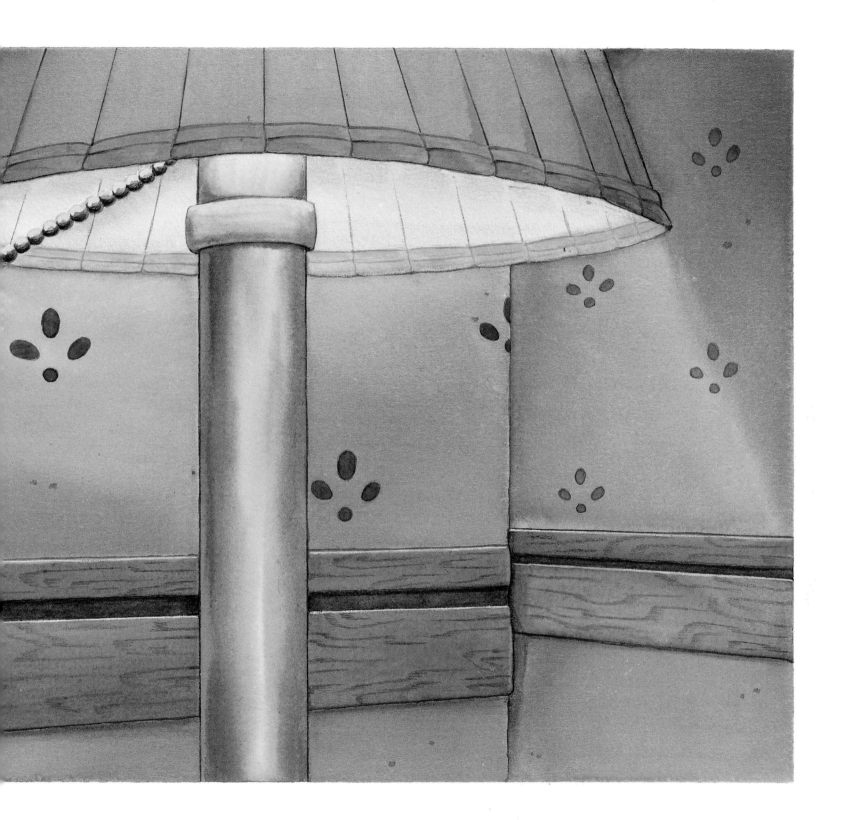

As George dropped to the floor, his giant shadow flew across the room, dark and scary.
The cat screeched—and bounded away.

The mice cheered for George and his giant shadow.
"You saved us, George!" they cried. "You're a hero!"

Then, the mice had a party to honor George. Everyone had lots of fun.

And from that day on, George, his giant shadow, and all the mice were the best of friends.